Diverting Devotion

by
Mike O'Malley

SAMUEL FRENCH

FOUNDED 1830

NEW YORK HOLLYWOOD LONDON TORONTO

SAMUELFRENCH.COM

ISBN 978-0-573-66034-4   Printed in U.S.A.   #6592

IMPORTANT BILLING AND CREDIT
REQUIREMENTS

DIVERTING DEVOTION premiered on March 16, 1996 at The Irish Arts Center in New York City. The production was Directed by Michael A. Mariano with the following cast:

PETER	Jack Mungovan
SULLY	Gerard O'Brien
CAROL	Catherine Mary Stewart
HENRY	Larry Clarke
JANICE	Dani Klein
NANCY	Kerry O'Malley
NICOLE	Catherine Corpeny

Stuart Rosenstein produced the premiere production of DIVERTING DEVOTION, with Scenic Design by Matthew Baird, Lighting Design by Deborah Constantine, and Sound Design by Eric Thompson. The Stage Manger was Amy Kiehl, the Assistant Director was Richard Munroe, and the Assistant Stage Manager was Peter Brydges. The production was cast by Mike Pepino and executive produced by Judy Mauer, Joel Feld, and Mike O'Malley.

DIVERTING DEVOTION was rewritten and produced by The Mineral Theatre Company at the Art/Works Theater in Los Angeles in November 2006. The production was Directed by Larry Clarke and was Produced by Jeffrey Donovan, Fielding Edlow and Mike O'Malley. The Stage Manager was Timothy O'Malley, with Lighting Design by Russell Boast, Scenic Design by Jeffrey Robinson, Sound design by Steve Altman, Fight Coordination by Jeffrey Donovan, and art designed for the production by Jon Leahy. Sally Shepard was the assistant stage manager, with the following cast:

PETER	Brendan O'Malley
SULLY	Michael Hurley
CAROL	Dee Ann Newkirk
HENRY	Terry Maratos
JANICE	Fielding Edlow
NANCY	Jen DeMartino
NICOLE	Melody Garren

This script is a rewrite of the original script, which was published by Samuel French in 1997.

CHARACTERS

PETER, 29
SULLY, 29
CAROL, 31
HENRY, 28
JANICE, 29
NANCY, 29
NICOLE, 29

TIME

The Present

SETTING

The majority of the action takes place on a Friday and Saturday in Peter's Manhattan apartment.

ACT ONE

Scene One

*(Lights up on Peter Callahan, 29, in his apartment on Manhattan's Upper West Side. He is reading a letter. His phone rings. In a separate space, the lights come up on Steve "**SULLY**" Sullivan, 29, in his house in Somerville, Massachusetts. **PETER** sees the Caller ID and answers.)*

PETER. Sully!

SULLY. Oh! The prodigal friend actually answered his phone!

PETER. Alright.

SULLY. "Alright, Sully's gonna give me a well-deserved ration of shit because I've kept him waitin' for a month to call him back, so I better just shut up and allow him to lay into me for bein' a negligent friend and makin' him feel like a *nuisance* for tryin' to finalize the plans for Fitzy's weddin' in *two weeks*."

PETER. I have been –

SULLY. "So I will suffer the shit Sully is slingin' in *silence* because Sully is *not* a nuisance, he's just a guy who is in a relationship with a woman who has expectations. *Reasonable* expectations which will not be met by Sully tellin' her that in regard to their trip to New York, they're gonna just *wing it*. Ah, yes. "Don't worry honey, if Pete doesn't get back to us, we can stay in a youth hostel."

PETER. The one on 14th is supposedly quite sanitary.

SULLY. Pete, I know it's difficult for someone immersed in a bachelor fog to fully grasp this, but my fiancee is an adult woman who likes to know what the *plan* is.

PETER. Yeah, no, I get it.

SULLY. When she travels to another city for a weddin' she likes to know where she is sleepin', and dinin', and if she needs to bring her own hair dryer – even though ultimately she will *always* bring her own hair dryer – she will still inquire about the availability of additional hair dryers because part of her process in puttin' together the days of her life is *makin' plans.*

PETER. I understand.

SULLY. Well, I'm not so sure you do. See, to make the plans she needs *information.* Information she will continue to seek until I give her enough *quality* information to make proper adult plans. Which I will give her once my friend Pete, who lives in the city where the weddin' is takin' place – and some months ago, offered up his apartment as lodgin' durin' that weddin' weekend – calls me back with the information!

PETER. You're right.

SULLY. Plans and information Pete. If you provide your lady with plans and information they will overlook all of your inferior attributes.

PETER. I shoulda called. You're right, every day I mean to call but I've just been –

SULLY. "Swamped." I know, you're so, so *swamped,* you're just, wow, I mean whoa, it's crazy how you can't squeak in four minutes to finalize an agenda with your best friend before he gets in his truck and drives down to that Sodom and Gomorrah of a city that in a swift two years has clearly corrupted you.

PETER. Sull, crash at my place, I'll get a pull-out.

SULLY. Don't sweat it, I booked a hotel in Times Square.

PETER. I need a new couch, I'll get it today.

SULLY. Lucky for you, Janice decided her pull-out couch days are over. But seriously, give me a good excuse for not returnin' one of the seven thousand messages I left.

PETER. I called to congratulate you on *your* engagement!

SULLY. *Called?* You mean your *text* of "Congrats!!" With two exclamation points and a smiley face guy? That call? Or that half-assed hieroglyphic you were kind enough to tap out in between naps?

PETER. I apologize.

SULLY. New York is warpin' your mind. You gotta get back to Boston. Save me from losin' *my* mind as I suffer through *my* weddin' plans.

PETER. I thought you weren't getting married 'til next year.

SULLY. If I make it through this one.

PETER. Plans and information?

SULLY. To a degree I was unaware was possible. It's not Janice, it's the *combination* of Janice with her Mother. Nothin' new, right? Moms, daughters, weddings, expectations... Seen it, heard about it, I think I got it covered because, I, The Smartest Groom Ever, will just *stay out of the way.*

PETER. Not possible.

SULLY. Not when important decisions have to be made like how the napkins will be folded. Should they be swans or Chinese fans? Let's spend *two weeks* comparin' and contrastin'! And cake designs! Butterflies or hydrangeas? Both are pretty! Back and forth, all day long. And then they go through the charade of askin' me *what I think* as if it's gonna impact the final decision. So I answer practically: *I don't care.* Which is the correct response if you wanna start a fight.

PETER. Good to know.

SULLY. I finally told Janice "You and your Mom need to place a little less importance on communication and a little more on shuttin' up."

PETER. How'd that go over?

SULLY. Great. She snapped, I apologized, makeup sex transpired, we went out to eat. It's the same sick dysfunction we've been cyclin' since high school. Somehow it works. Although takin' Janice to Burger King no longer flies.

Dependin' on how insensitive I was, I gotta spring for either Panera or The Cheesecake Factory.

(Call waiting interrupts them.)

PETER. Hold on, it's Carol.

SULLY. Go.

*(***PETER*** switches over and finds **CAROL** Powers, 31. She is calling from a movie set in Vancouver.)*

PETER. Carol?

CAROL. Hi! Is something wrong?

PETER. No, no – I'm sorry – I just got Sully on the other line.

CAROL. Which one's Sully again?

PETER. My old roommate.

CAROL. From college or after college?

PETER. Both.

CAROL. You mean that guy in the picture on your fridge with the neck thing you guys do?

PETER. No, that's Tom Welch.

CAROL. Can you call him back? I'm on a quick break.

PETER. Don't go anywhere.

*(He clicks back over to **SULLY**.)*

PETER. Yo. I gotta hop. Carol's in Vancouver on set –

SULLY. Carol? Been seein' her for a while, huh? Good for you.

PETER. Can I call you right back?

SULLY. *(serious)* Yeah, Pete, real quick. Fitzy called me and, uh – well, I wanted to pass on the information that uh, Nicole's goin' to be there at his weddin'.

*(***PETER*** glances at the letter he holds in his hand.)*

SULLY. Fitz, you know…I guess he felt he had to invite her because they were friends too – whatever – we all were, I don't have to school you. He didn't think she'd actually travel all the way back to the States, but, she is – so, sorry to drop the bomb. I know it sucks wicked but –

PETER. No, Sull, thanks for the heads-up.

SULLY. And since I knew Fitz' future in-laws are only lettin' married or engaged people bring dates, that you wouldn't be able to parade around some babe to make it clear to Nicole that you're better off without her – so I thought you should know. To get your head warmed up to seein' her there. And so did Fitz. He doesn't know all the details that I do, but he still knows it might be awkward. I told him I'd call you. He's got enough stuff goin' on right now.

PETER. Right.

SULLY. Pete, all I wanna say is – don't let it faze you buddy, it'll be fine. We'll just stake out our own space, hang with the boys, and abuse alcohol in a stereotypical way. Henry's goin', right?

PETER. He's calling around looking to borrow a suit.

SULLY. You get a last minute invite to the rehearsal dinner?

PETER. Didn't make the cut.

SULLY. Neither did I. Fitz's got too many cousins that have priority. So let's meet up Friday night in the city and grab dinner.

PETER. Done.

SULLY. Look at that! A plan! Two weeks pal. We will rage. Fitzy's gettin' hitched! Don't bail on me.

PETER. I won't.

SULLY. That's what you said about his bachelor party.

PETER. See you in two weeks.

SULLY. Peace.

(Lights down on Sully. **PETER**, *oblivious to the fact that Carol's still on the other line, hangs up. It immediately rings, and as he picks it up, the lights come up on* **CAROL**, *who is understandably, miffed.)*

PETER. Carol?

CAROL. Pete, what was *that*?

PETER. I'm sorry.

CAROL. That wasn't very nice.

PETER. You're right.

CAROL. I told you I had a quick break!

PETER. Sorry.

CAROL. It's just, sometimes it seems we've hardly spoken since I've been here. It's just, voice-mail to voice-mail and texting little snippets and you hate the e-mail thing so I don't get the day-to-day stuff –

PETER. Carol, you're on a film set, with new people in a fun city –

CAROL. Be more fun with you.

PETER. You're doing something new every day. I'm doing the same boring stuff that's not worth detailing.

CAROL. Sorry, I'm just overworked and under-appreciated.

PETER. Oh, is that all?

CAROL. The actress playing Lucy keeps complaining about how all the special makeup I'm applying to her face *itches.* I wanna say "Hey dummy, shoulda thought about that before you took the part of a *burn victim!*"

PETER. You should.

CAROL. That'd get me sent home sooner. Six weeks is too long to be away.

PETER. I'm sorry I forgot about you on the other line.

CAROL. I'll let it slip. This time. Okay. I gotta go. I'm looking forward to not having to say that anymore.

PETER. Two weeks!

CAROL. Twelve days! I'll call later, but E-mail me! I love you.

PETER. I love you too.

(CAROL and PETER hang up their phones. PETER looks at the letter. Lights down.)

Scene Two

(PETER answers the door as HENRY Vataha, 28, enters, thumbing his cellphone.)

PETER. Buzzer broke again?

HENRY. Door too.

PETER. I was just down there and it was working fine. This neighborhood, I'm telling you.

(PETER hands HENRY a pair of black shoes.)

HENRY. You got any brown ones?

PETER. What?

HENRY. The suit my uncle gave me ended up being brown. Black with brown? Not good.

PETER. How does a 28 year-old man not own a pair of dress shoes?

HENRY. When I finish my novel, you will read it, and the answer to that question – and others that may very well save humanity – will be revealed to you.

(PETER exits to the bedroom.)

HENRY. Place is looking spiffy. You hire a maid?

PETER. (O.S.) I can clean my own apartment.

HENRY. Short on cash?

(PETER reenters carrying some brown shoes.)

PETER. I'm a grown man.

HENRY. Nice to finally meet one.

(PETER hands him the shoes.)

HENRY. Thanks. And hey, since you're saving on a maid, this may be a good time to bridge my request for some, how should I put it? Some money.

PETER. The shoes were a decoy?

HENRY. There's many areas in which I need assistance. But I also came by to visit, and, and to welcome Carol back to town.

PETER. She's grabbing some stuff at her apartment.

HENRY. I know this sounds stupid, but my bank card's on the blink.

PETER. How much do you need?

HENRY. My secret code got erased when I put it down on the counter at the bookstore.

PETER. Hank –

HENRY. I put it down on some magnetic security clearance pad by the cashier that was camouflaged by this wood paneling paint! It wiped out the info on my card, it's Friday night, the bank's closed, I'm screwed. I would get a cash advance on a credit card, but as of last month, I'm in a debit-only situation.

PETER. Will a hundred work?

HENRY. Not as well as three.

PETER. Hank, you're not gonna be able to buy a suit and get it tailored by tomorrow night!

HENRY. I told you, my uncle hooked me with a suit. I need the float for *tonight.*

PETER. I'll cover you at dinner.

HENRY. I'm gonna meet you later. I'm having dinner at Gotham.

PETER. I'm not letting you blow three hundred at that place.

HENRY. Women need to be impressed now and then.

PETER. Since when does Chelsea like places like that?

HENRY. You mean Chesley?

PETER. Why do I still do that? Sorry, Chesley.

HENRY. Don't be, we're ovs.

PETER. What?

HENRY. As of Tuesday night, over, ovs. Thirsty?

(**HENRY** *grabs a soda from an offstage fridge.*)

PETER. All you have to say is "ovs?"

HENRY. Exactly. I have nothing else to say about a woman who had nothing to say.

PETER. That isn't true.

HENRY. Kinda is. In fact, I wouldn't be surprised if at one point the contents of her head had been erased by that pad at the bookstore.

PETER. That's a little harsh.

HENRY. It's my exit interview summation. 'Course it's harsh. I can move on faster if I focus on her flaws.

PETER. What'd she say?

HENRY. Oh, it was awesome. "You smell, you suck in bed, the pock marks on your forehead are more noticeable than you think, so pay me what you owe me and get out of my apartment before I cry rape, you sad, sad excuse for a man."

PETER. Musta been hard to break it to her.

HENRY. *She* broke up with *me*.

PETER. What? And still said all that?

HENRY. I think she was so used to getting crushed by all her previous boyfriends that she was beside herself with giddy rage that *she* finally got to do the crushing. Went kinda overboard, if you ask me, but I can handle it.

PETER. Sorry you're going through that.

HENRY. Don't be. I schemed for this. Been laying the groundwork for *weeks*.

(A beat.)

PETER. You can be exhausting to follow. Back up a second.

HENRY. I wanted *her* to end it. So about two weeks ago I set it in motion. Stopped showering. Laid around her apartment. Left dirty plates everywhere. Left my wet towel on the bed, coffee cup on the back of the toilet, that kinda shit. Ate entire meals standing up. Over the sink. On the floor. In the bed. Didn't pull any garden variety Lothario shit. Just did some specific inconsiderate lazy guy shit. Women in their late twenties, early thirties – they can't STAND that.

PETER. Why didn't you just break up with her?

HENRY. Nah. I can't initiate breakups anymore. Too much emotional…*reverberation*. Even if it's good for them – they can't see it. You say some lame intangible thing like "It's not working out," and that just triggers the reawakening of all this bad stuff left in…*hibernation* from guys who broke their hearts in the past.

PETER. Yeah.

HENRY. You gotta tread lightly with the late twenties, early thirties female. If you carelessly pile onto her romantic history just another generic douchebag guy break-up, you run the risk of turning that woman into a hater of our entire gender. No one wants that. You gotta leave them some room to believe in trying again with someone more suitable. Basically, it's my way of looking out for my fellow man by doing everything in my power to get *women* to do the abandoning.

PETER. *(Deadpan)* Our grateful gender thanks you.

HENRY. Believe me, I want something to work, to last, to be authentic and as real as much as anybody else does. Problem is, it takes *months* before you get to someone's true nature. And by that time, you've had way too many conversations about the future and way too much sex to just say, "Sorry, I'm kinda done here." I've been there, I've done that. It's cruel. While you're trying to end things cordially, they start reciting all the stuff you said or did that made you seem like you liked them, which you *did*, before you got to know them, and realize you don't like 'em like in a *forever* way. They start saying things like "You imposter!" Remember Janey? She beat that word into the ground. "You're an *IMPOSTER!*" And then the whole sorry aftermath with the late night calls and the tears – it's exhausting. And I've been on the receiving end too, so, I know what blind-siding does to a person's psyche. This way it's like giving them a gift. This way – revealing yourself to be a lazy, smelly, shiftless guy – this way they feel *courageous* for getting rid of you. They feel like they're taking charge of their life by removing from their life a man who clearly cannot provide. They feel assertive and empowered. Me, I get liberation and no bad aftertaste.

PETER. I wished things worked that way for everyone.

HENRY. I am proof that they can. And the thing is, I was rewarded immediately for my gift-giving to Chesley, because, the moment I walked out of her place I saw this shapely chick reading "Middlemarch" in Central Park, and I tell ya Pete, I don't miss a step. I go right into my thing, referencing this character and that, dropping insightful, well-honed opinions about John Raffles and Caleb Garth. Next thing you know, she gives me her number. And we're dining tonight at Gotham. Should be fun to date old school. You know? See girl, chat her up, blow her mind with the expanse of my own – and then – ask on date. At least then there's some mystery involved. With Chesley, I just scanned her profile online, and jumped to conclusions: "She's likes Wilco, she's a vegan, we're *alike! I'll send her a Superpoke and see what transpires.*" Ugh. Lesson learned. Lesson *mastered.* But this new one tonight, this lovely woman, this reader of century old fiction, has, in five minutes in the park, given every indication she could be a blue chipper. So, you know, could I borrow your bank card?

PETER. Yeah.

HENRY. So, what's with you? You thinking about breaking up with Carol?

PETER. Why do you say that?

HENRY. "Yes" is a shorter answer.

*(As the lights come down on **PETER** and **HENRY**, they both remain on-stage. The lights then come up on **SULLY** and his fiancee, **JANICE** Mariano, 29, driving in their car.)*

SULLY. Pete's my best friend JANICE!

JANICE. I'm not arguing that.

SULLY. I'm not gonna scratch Pete, especially if I have to be standin' up on the altar with your two brothers and your sister's dirtbag husband!

JANICE. Tony's not a dirtbag.

SULLY. Yeah, only certifiable good guys leave their wives on I-95 in a blizzard.

JANICE. For five minutes. He was trying to scare her.

SULLY. He succeeded.

JANICE. Melanie dug herself that hole.

SULLY. By stickin' up for herself?

JANICE. By spitting in his face.

SULLY. He completely overreacted.

JANICE. I wasn't there.

SULLY. Like you wouldn't call me a dirtbag if I left you on the interstate in a blizzard?

JANICE. You wouldn't do that.

SULLY. Well, people change. *(Off her)* Not me. But other people. I can't believe your brothers didn't knock his teeth out.

JANICE. My brothers lift their asses off the couch? Their heads would explode from the change in altitude.

SULLY. Which brings me to my original point. If I gotta stand on the altar next to Tony and those two idiots, I want somebody along with my brother, and Pete's my best friend.

JANICE. But then there'd be five on your side, four on mine.

SULLY. Correct.

JANICE. It wouldn't be the same.

SULLY. Four and five are different numbers, yes.

JANICE. It wouldn't be even.

SULLY. So what?

JANICE. It matters!

SULLY. *(laughing)* Define "matters."

JANICE. Organization. Symmetry. The composition of the photos that we'll be looking at for the rest of our lives.

SULLY. Then add somebody to your side.

JANICE. You don't just add somebody to make a photo look better.

SULLY. You don't subtract somebody either.

JANICE. You can't subtract somebody that wasn't up there in the first place.

SULLY. I didn't realize I had to submit paperwork on my groomsmen for a symmetry check! I mean good God, this is ridiculous!

JANICE. Yeah, why am I planning all of this? Nobody cares how it looks.

SULLY. Not symmetry!

JANICE. Let's forget the flowers, the candles, the tuxes.

SULLY. Sure, save some money.

JANICE. Hell, forget my wedding dress! Let's get married in t-shirts and cut-offs!

SULLY. Janice –

JANICE. We'll have a cook out, a pot-luck supper! You can wear your flip-flops while you work the grill! I'll tap the kegs and my brothers will bring the bottle rockets!

SULLY. Sweet. I'll look into rentin' out Fenway.

(Lights down on SULLY *and* JANICE, *and back up on* PETER *and* HENRY.*)*

*(*PETER *pulls out his wallet.)*

HENRY. So you dropping the hammer on her tonight?

(A beat.)

PETER. I'm just, ya know, thinking through some –

HENRY. *(sincere)* Pete, you're skittish and distracted. You get strange whenever any of our friends get married and you're getting strange now. When our friends get married, you start thinking about life, and the long term, and Nicole and what happened. And you compare. You consider where you should be and who you should be with. Nicole's hard to compare to. You also find it difficult to hurt people. Which is what makes you a great guy. But one wrong thing happening once in your life does not mean you have to be overly cautious about being right the rest of your life. *(Beat)* You want to talk about it?

PETER. No.

HENRY. Good, 'cause that was pretty much all I got.

(**HENRY** *holds up the bank card.*)

HENRY. *(sincere)* You always help me out. I appreciate that.

PETER. You've been there for me plenty of times.

HENRY. Uh, Pete? This is some frequent flyer card.

(**PETER** *takes the card back.*)

PETER. You know what? Let's hit my ATM, I gotta pick up some stuff before Sully and Janice get here anyway.

HENRY. Sully and Janice. That's cool they're going the distance too. Good to see you guys still in touch. That's cool man. Cool shit.

(**CAROL** *enters, a bit rushed, with a towel around her head.*)

CAROL. Are they here?

PETER. No, only Henry.

CAROL. Hey, Henry!

(*They hug.*)

HENRY. Carol, I like the new look.

CAROL. Wrong time to joke about the wrong thing, Henry! My flight was three hours late, and I'm about to meet Sully and Janice for the first time and I look horrible.

(*She rushes into the bathroom.*)

HENRY. *(to* **PETER***)* It'll be easier than you think.

(*They exit as the lights come up on* **SULLY** *and* **JANICE**, *on the road to New York.*)

JANICE. Why don't we have Peter do a reading?

SULLY. I'm not going to half-ass his participation with some crap role.

JANICE. Doing a reading is an *honor.* Besides, all the readers get to go to the rehearsal dinner, and he'll have an immediate bond with Shawna since she's doing a reading too, and they can sit together and who knows, maybe love will bloom.

SULLY. No, I told you, he's got a steady girlfriend now.

JANICE. Since when?

SULLY. Since a while.

JANICE. You never told me this.

SULLY. Yes I did. He's been seein' her for about a year.

JANICE. Seriously?

SULLY. Yes.

JANICE. No, I mean are they dating seriously?

SULLY. They've been datin' for a year.

JANICE. When did you tell me this?

SULLY. A while ago. Her name's Carol…used to be an actress, now she's a makeup artist on movies…is it comin' back to you? You know, memory loss is becomin' a stark side effect from your little dope smokin' renaissance.

JANICE. Don't even start.

SULLY. Are you holdin' right now?

JANICE. No.

SULLY. Me being a cop doesn't get you a free pass if you get caught with it by some other cops. And people *do* get caught. All the time. And when you come cryin' to me, I won't be able to fix it.

JANICE. I'll just take off my shirt. Worked before.

(He looks at her. She laughs.)

SULLY. I wasn't buyin' it.

JANICE. There was a moment you thought *maybe…*

SULLY. You're too Catholic.

JANICE. Not always.

SULLY. Don't carry that stuff when you're drivin'. House only.

JANICE. Yessir officer.

SULLY. And now that you've put the subject on my mind, how about you give a little lift there?

JANICE. What?

SULLY. Flash me.

JANICE. Stop.

SULLY. Give a man a thrill while he's stuck in traffic.

JANICE. Like you said, I'm Catholic. It's too late to start acting like a rest stop whore.

SULLY. I'll be the judge of that. C'mon, out with 'em.

(Lights down.)

(Lights up at the Gotham Cafe, where HENRY *sits opposite his date,* NANCY *Rogers, 29. They are holding menus.)*

HENRY. So…What are you having?

NANCY. Hmm. Salad. Maybe. Maybe a sandwich. I don't know. Gazpacho. Blah. Watercress? Yuck. Doubt it. You ever have watercress?

HENRY. No.

NANCY. Fucking sucks shit.

(A beat.)

HENRY. Really?

NANCY. Is lettuce such a problem? Is regular iceberg lettuce such a fucking problem?

HENRY. I'm sure if you requested –

NANCY. No, we gotta get all fucking fancy with the fucking *watercress!* Look at this place. "Grilled pear and brie?" As a sandwich? Fucking doubt it! I'm so sick of this shit. It really bugs me when some Food Network wannabe creates arbitrary bullshit sandwiches just to show off how he can mix up random shit from his fridge and then charges the fuck out of his customers so he can cover the overhead he brought upon himself by decorating the bathrooms with vintage fucking formica.

HENRY. There's probably some feedback cards you can fill out –

NANCY. *(muttering)* It's like "Fuck you motherfucker. Fuck you and your fourteen dollar watercress-sundried-tomato-ginger sprinkled-seven grained sack of shit sandwich."

HENRY. I hear ya.

NANCY. How about a turkey fucking club? Toasted white bread, turkey, bacon, mayo. I mean, What. The. Fuck?

(A beat.)

HENRY. You wanna go to a different restaurant?

NANCY. I'll cope. But first I'm gonna kill a cigarette. You smoke?

HENRY. No.

NANCY. Well, if it's an issue, we better cut bait right here.

HENRY. Cut bait?

NANCY. I like to smoke. I like the thought of carcinogens coating my lungs and the rest of my innards with a black tar-like substance that may bring about violent pain and misery thirty years from now. Live and let die! It's my one vice. I do yoga, I run, and I don't wear makeup except for a little cruelty-free eyeliner on the nights I actually leave my apartment. People don't like it, tough shit. Fuckholes can fuck off.

HENRY. I admire your candor. So. How long you been teaching third grade?

(Lights down on HENRY and NANCY, and back up on SULLY and JANICE, still driving. JANICE is adjusting her bra.)

JANICE. What's she like?

SULLY. What?

JANICE. The woman who's dating Pete, what's she like?

SULLY. Sorry. Your decision to finally flash me has put my mind in other places.

JANICE. Is she nice, pretty?

SULLY. Never met her.

JANICE. They've been dating a while, and you've never met her?

SULLY. When would I have met her?

JANICE. I just think it's weird that your best friend has been dating a woman for a while, and you've never met her.

SULLY. Yeah, pretty weird Janice, huh? Pretty spooky weird.

JANICE. Just saying –

SULLY. Janice, they've been datin' a while, I've not been down to New York for a while, Pete hasn't been back to Boston, I don't see the hard-to-unravel riddle.

JANICE. Am I going to meet her tonight?

SULLY. I guess.

JANICE. Is she going to the wedding tomorrow?

SULLY. Only married or engaged people can bring a date.

JANICE. I bet if he was still dating Nicole he could bring *her.*

SULLY. Nicole was Fitzy's friend too, so it doesn't matter.

JANICE. I can't believe she's coming back.

SULLY. Gotta lotta gall.

JANICE. Is Pete over Nicole?

SULLY. He's datin' somebody else.

JANICE. That doesn't mean anything.

SULLY. Means enough.

JANICE. I never really got them.

SULLY. Nicole and Pete? They were great together! If she didn't wig out on him we'd be drivin' to *their* weddin'.

JANICE. You don't know that.

SULLY. She wigged. That's the problem with women. Not you. But *other* women are always complainin' about how they can't find a great guy, then they find one like Pete and sabotage the whole thing. They were awesome together. *(Beat)* Course we can't tell Pete that anymore. Bygones are bygones, she's gone, he's moved on. He's got a new girl. We gotta support him, not remind him of the past.

JANICE. Are we going to let him bring this Carol person to our wedding?

SULLY. Janice, please –

JANICE. I know, but I'd like to finalize the list.

SULLY. You promised we'd take the weekend off from discussin' it!

JANICE. It's not an easy promise to follow through on.

SULLY. Please, can we just get through one weddin' at a time? Let's just get to New York and enjoy Fitzy's weddin' and then we'll work on ours. I need a break. I need a break from the lists, the magazines, the books, and my head hurts so much I'm about to shoot myself.

JANICE. You didn't bring it, did you?

(SULLY nods.)

JANICE. You actually brought your gun? Why? What for?

SULLY. Bad things happen in the big city, Jan. You gotta be prepared.

(Lights down. Lights back up on NANCY and HENRY.)

NANCY. How long have I been teaching? Too long. Is it something I still leap out of bed to do? Doubt it. You can't even call it teaching. More like babysitting the future Hitler Youth of the Tri-State Area. I used to have visions of some disaffected inner city class with me at the helm, *bestowing knowledge.* I was gonna "make a difference!" Doubt it! Fuck teaching. I am so fucking done.

HENRY. Well said. What new industry will be the beneficiary of your skill-set?

NANCY. Who the fuck knows? I've been saying I'm gonna quit for three years. Still got seven months of this year's sorry ass shit. I don't now. I've always wanted to try massage therapy.

HENRY. Really?

NANCY. What's that look for?

HENRY. What look?

NANCY. You think that means your night's gonna end with a lower-waist handshake?

HENRY. I'm not sure I know what that is.

NANCY. Doubt it. I know the look, so bag it. And bag the puppy dog reaction too.

(**HENRY** *stands. He's more baffled than angry.*)

HENRY. You know, I'm actually gonna bag more than that.

NANCY. *(softening)* Where are you going?

HENRY. Away?

NANCY. Sit back down.

HENRY. *(a plea)* I'm uncomfortable.

NANCY. Please. I know, you're thinking, "She's swearing, she's a pig. Fuck this." Let me explain myself... *(Sincerely)* Really. I'm over-doing the swearing because –

HENRY. No, that's not why –

NANCY. Please.

HENRY. It's why.

(**HENRY** *sits.*)

NANCY. I'm overdoing the swearing because I want people to see my worst case scenario from the get-go. Indisputably, my worst personality trait is the potential I have, to *at times,* use gutter terms when they are not at all necessary. When you've got three brothers, the gutter mouth gets handed down like an old pair of ice skates, and it's a real shitty thing to lay on your little sister, but fuck it, at this point, I'm fucked. I express myself with profane terms at times and I'm trying to fix that, but meanwhile, I got it – it's like a speech impediment that's hard to shake – and I needed you to know up-front that I'm not just the woman who reads books like "Middlemarch."

HENRY. Oh, we have surely eclipsed the first impression.

NANCY. That first impression wasn't a lie, though! It was a true component of me...But, see, there's other stuff to who I am. Good and bad. And my last boyfriend left me because he said I became somebody different when we moved in together. His laundry list started with what he called my "thirst for vulgarity," but the truth is he just didn't have the sack to communicate and then stay, to be honest but not flee, to work through things, to let me improve my language arts, to see me as someone

who could change for the better. He thought the definition of commitment meant "Hang out 'til you get
bored, fed up or find something better." Fucking dick.
Fuck him!

HENRY. Uh-huh.

NANCY. So here I am. My worst character trait out in the
open. Yes, I've got work to do, we've all got work to
do, but the point is, I don't have time to get involved
in a relationship that is just a disease in its incubation
stage. Here's who I am sometimes. We live in a profane
world and I, at times, unfortunately, am a reflection of
it. Fact is, the majority of the time I'm a lot of fun.

HENRY. When's that side start showing?

NANCY. I admit this is completely unorthodox, but I've con-
cluded that it's important to show the parts you're not
necessarily proud of *right away*. But I still, you know,
want to meet someone and I don't – That was the first
time I've tried something like that.

HENRY. You really committed!

NANCY. You're thinking I might be whacked in the head,
huh?

HENRY. Oh, I *know* you're whacked in the head. No further
evaluation necessary. Fortunately for you, I'm whacked
too. I dig honesty, bare bonesin' it. I dig openness. I
dig taking chances. You?

NANCY. Yeah…I think I might try the watercress after all…
Ready to order?

HENRY. Fuck yeah. Where's that fuckin' waiter?

(Lights down.)

Scene Three

*(**CAROL** enters from the bedroom with her hair in a funky headband. She's on the phone.)*

CAROL. Hey Rachel – I'm back! Listen, I know we have plans for lunch Monday, but that might change...I'll tell you the details when you call me back, but basically – I found a print-out for a reservation in Pete's name at a Bed and Breakfast in Nantucket for this Monday and Tuesday! So, what you said last week could be right! *(Giddy)* Ahh! Okay, I gotta stay composed. I mean I didn't find a *ring*. And even if I did, I – well – I wouldn't be able to contain myself – besides, I can't even tell him I was rifling around his stuff looking for shoe polish because – he's coming in – I'll call you as soon as I know something!

*(**PETER** enters carrying beers.)*

CAROL. Ta-da! How do I look?

PETER. Wow.

CAROL. Is it bad?

PETER. What? No.

CAROL. I was trying something different. It's bad, isn't it?

PETER. You look great.

CAROL. Shit, shit, I wanted to try to be a bit more festive.

(She pulls off the headband.)

PETER. Carol, you look beautiful.

CAROL. It's so great to be back. Kiss. Kiss kiss kiss. *(Smothering him with kisses)* Oh, I can't believe we have no alone time today. I missed you. I wish I was going with you to the wedding.

PETER. Listen, Carol –

CAROL. *(sweet)* I understand. They don't know me, they shouldn't waste a spot. There's all their college friends they want there. Besides, I need a day to get re-situated.

(There's a banging on the door.)

CAROL. Oh, that must be them!

*(**PETER** opens the door, and **SULLY** and **JANICE** enter.)*

PETER. Welcome!

SULLY. Yo stranger!

(They shake hands and hug.)

PETER. Hi Janice!

JANICE. Hi Peter!

CAROL. Hi!

PETER. Guys, this is Carol.

SULLY. Hi Carol!

JANICE. Hi, I'm Janice!

*(**CAROL** hugs her, then **SULLY**.)*

CAROL. Hi! And this is the famous Sully! Welcome to New York!!

SULLY. Thanks! Sorry we're a little late. 95 was a parkin' lot.

PETER. It's good to see you.

*(**SULLY** makes himself at home, checking the place out.)*

SULLY. Big man in the Big Apple. Look at this place. Not bad. About the size of my bathroom. But, high ceilings…

*(He steps into Peter's bedroom offstage. **PETER** follows.)*

SULLY. (O.S.) Look at Mr. Crafty! You make that loft yourself?

PETER. (O.S.) Need all the space you can get.

(They reenter.)

SULLY. Too high for me. That is not a ladder to climb drunk. Someone could get hurt.

PETER. Speaking of which, what's with your hand?

*(**PETER** points to a bandage on Sully's hand.)*

SULLY. Took a detour through some lowlife's face.

CAROL. Law and order takes some effort, huh?

JANICE. *(scoffs)* Oh, please.

SULLY. I got in a little donnybrook at the Pats game. Some drunken lowlife at the tailgate grabbed Janice's ass. Right in front of me, grabbed a big chunk of her ass.

JANICE. Big chunk?

SULLY. I embellish for the entertainment value.

JANICE. I appreciate the clarification.

CAROL. Want some Advil?

SULLY. No thanks Carol, I'm fine. Besides, I'll be liquored up in about an hour with this man leadin' the way… but, hey, it's great to meet you finally!

CAROL. I know, I've heard so much about you both! Congratulations on your engagement!

SULLY. We're all droppin' like flies.

JANICE. Marvelous.

CAROL. Janice, your ring, I can see from here, it's so beautiful.

JANICE. Thank you.

PETER. Beer?

SULLY. Am I breathin'?

PETER. Janice, beer?

JANICE. Sure, thanks Pete.

CAROL. You know what Peter? What the hell? Me too.

PETER. Done.

(**PETER** *exits to the kitchen.*)

CAROL. When's the wedding?

JANICE. I don't have permission to talk about it.

SULLY. Now who's embarrassin' who?

JANICE. Hey, I don't want any shots fired.

SULLY. I didn't say we couldn't answer *general* questions about it.

CAROL. Did I bring up the wrong topic?

JANICE. We've been having a lot of drama with the planning and Steve – we – decided to take a weekend break from discussing it.

CAROL. Oh, I feel horrible for even bringing –

SULLY. We can talk about it!

JANICE. Good. *(To* CAROL*)* We've narrowed it down to two dates next July. We're still deciding. Our list is like, ever-expanding.

(**PETER** *reenters and distributes the beers.)*

PETER. You guys have friends?

SULLY. Her father has friends.

JANICE. My father is footing the bill.

SULLY. Because he invited every drywaller in Boston.

JANICE. Drywall is what put me through school.

SULLY. *(to* PETER*)* Yeah, and drywall is what I put you through at "Paddy Burke's," remember that?

PETER. No, you threw me headfirst. There was lasting damage.

CAROL. It's hard to do the list, huh?

JANICE. The place we want only holds three hundred.

SULLY. Of our *closest* friends.

JANICE. You'd be surprised how many friends you accumulate by the time you're thirty.

CAROL. My sister had a hard time with her list.

JANICE. People I didn't even know I was related to started appearing out of thin air. Then you got stragglers like my mother's college roommate. Yeah, can't wait to see her!

SULLY. Course on the bright side, we're talkin' a boatload of presents.

JANICE. I'll admit, my Mom's completely over the top.

SULLY. A breakthrough! Janice!

JANICE. *(ignoring)* But I'm the only girl, so –

CAROL. She wants to do it big, I totally understand.

SULLY. Walk a mile, Carol. Walk a mile in my Rockports and then we'll reconvene.

JANICE. Excuse me, where's the bathroom?

CAROL. Right down the hall, second door on the left.

(*JANICE exits to the bathroom.*)

CAROL. *(sincere)* I just think it's great how you're gonna make this commitment to one another and your future starts having some shape to it. You're able to say, "Okay, this is what we're gonna be doing. We're gonna walk hand-in-hand together." And give some, you know, some meaning that you can grab hold of that's *definitive*. That's really touching – it always gets me – when two people say yes to step up a commitment. It's sweet.

(*A beat. SULLY nods, as does PETER.*)

SULLY. Yeah. Honestly, I don't want to give the wrong impression. I'm excited about *bein'* married. Gettin' married? I know this is not an original conclusion for a man to put forth, it's just – when you're in it – Every free half second I'm scurryin' around town tryin' to find a photographer, a band, a banquet hall. It's like a second job! I've been to the tuxedo shop, goin' on six times – first, just gettin' a tux – then, gettin' a tux with tails, then a top hat. Don't ask me why, I guess Janice has the hots for Abe Lincoln, but hey – I love the tux shop! Did you know cummerbunds are back and vests are out? I do. I've tried on some cummerbunds. I've chosen some cummerbunds. I've had my *chosen* cummerbund changed every time Janice changes the color of her bridesmaids' dresses –

(*JANICE reenters.*)

JANICE. I've changed it once.

SULLY. Twice.

JANICE. Okay twice.

SULLY. *(To CAROL and PETER)* It just gets to be a pain in the ass. *(To JANICE)* And I know it's nobody's fault. And heck, it'll pay off, which is the important thing.

JANICE. We just wanna get everything out of the way so we can enjoy the week before, and the actual day.

CAROL. You don't wanna be stressed about little things.

SULLY. Right. I wanna be stressed out about big things like, "Why the hell am I marryin' *her?*"

(Daggers from **JANICE**. **SULLY** *points to* **CAROL**.*)*

SULLY. C'mon, she teed that up. It was reflexive.

CAROL. Peter told me that you guys were high school sweethearts. That's great!

SULLY. *(sincere)* It's beyond great!

JANICE. Go ahead, dig yourself out.

SULLY. It's the best! This day and age, havin' a history with somebody helps, you know?

JANICE. Keep going.

SULLY. Old ties, roots, knowin' who people are and what they're about.

JANICE. How far they've come, how far they still have to go.

SULLY. Touche.

CAROL. How'd you finally know it was time?

SULLY. No big reason. Time to either shit or get off the pot.

JANICE. That's lovely.

SULLY. What?

JANICE. Equating your proposal to a bowel movement.

SULLY. Alright –

JANICE. Your metaphor for getting engaged is *taking a shit?*

(A beat.)

SULLY. Sometimes takin' a shit feels good.

JANICE. I don't want to be compared to a shit being taken!

SULLY. I wasn't –

JANICE. You said the same thing to two people on the phone yesterday! Can't you ever say "I realized I couldn't live without her!"?

SULLY. Janice –

JANICE. Instead, I get the equivalent of, "It was time to take a dump." "When ya gotta pinch one, ya pinch one!"

SULLY. *(To* **PETER** *and* **CAROL***)* We had a long ride down –

JANICE. "Had to lay some cable!" "Time to cop a squat!"

SULLY. Okay, now you're the one who's goin' off!

JANICE. Once, just *once*, I'd like to hear you say "I love her! I'm crazy about her! I realized I couldn't live without her!"

(A beat.)

SULLY.*(sincere)* I do love you. I am crazy about you. I don't even want to consider livin' without you. I'm sorry. It's a stupid phrase to describe an awesome thing. I will never utter it again. I'm sorry.

JANICE. I'm sorry too.

(They kiss. Then, a bit embarrassed, they turn to **PETER** *and* **CAROL***.)*

JANICE/SULLY. Sorry you guys.

PETER. No problem.

SULLY. We never get like this.

JANICE. That was rude of us.

CAROL. No –

PETER. Guys, really –

JANICE. It was rude and childish. Sorry.

SULLY. Carol, we haven't made a very good first impression huh?

CAROL. Reminds me of growing up.

(A beat.)

JANICE. Oh? I'm sorry.

CAROL. No, I'm fine. It's fine. I'm okay.

(Awkward moment.)

*(***PETER** *stands, trying to change the mood.)*

PETER. *(to* **SULLY***)* Tell you what – why don't we sit outside on the fire escape with these stogies I picked up to celebrate your engagement?

CAROL. Won't that ruin your tastebuds before dinner?

SULLY. The alcohol will have the same impact, so six of one, half dozen of the other. *(To* **JANICE***)* Come 'ere.

(**SULLY** *bear-hugs* **JANICE.**)

PETER.*(to* **CAROL***)* Just give us twenty minutes to smoke these and then we'll go.

CAROL. Okay stinky smoke man, but you better brush your teeth if you're gonna kiss me.

JANICE. Peter, is there a drugstore around here?

CAROL. Yeah, two blocks south.

JANICE. Left or right out the front?

PETER. Left.

SULLY. You okay?

JANICE. Me – yeah. But since you guys are gonna smoke, I thought, well, the toilet paper ran out –

CAROL.*(Embarrassed)* I am so sorry.

SULLY. *(joking, to* **PETER***) That* is so rude! I can't believe you!

PETER. That's my fault Janice –

JANICE. I got the tail end. Let me go get more.

PETER. No, no way, I'll go.

SULLY. Giddy up pal, I'm crowning.

JANICE. Allow me to go, if only as an excuse to get away from that creature for a few moments.

SULLY. Now, now.

JANICE. Besides, I promised myself that this trip I'd see something in Manhattan other than the inside of a bar.

CAROL. No problem, I'll take you.

(*They exit.*)

SULLY. Pick up some of those adult wipes!

JANICE. (O.S.) Go smoke!

SULLY. You tried those?

PETER. What?

SULLY. Moist adult wipes. It's like a moist wipe for a baby's butt, but for adults. Janice started buyin' them recently, and honestly, I don't know how I ever lived without 'em.

(A beat.)

PETER. I'll check 'em out.

SULLY. It'll change your life. The way you feel afterward –

PETER. Yeah, I get the concept.

SULLY. Sorry about the, uh – discussion you had to witness.

PETER. Not a problem.

SULLY. It's a little tense sometimes.

PETER. Yeah?

SULLY. The finality of it all.

PETER. Yeah.

SULLY. But it's good.

PETER. Yup.

SULLY. Puts you to the test, you know?

PETER. Apparently so.

*(**SULLY** laughs.)*

SULLY. So many people gettin' married.

PETER. Uh-huh.

SULLY. Carol seems nice.

*(**PETER** nods.)*

SULLY. Do not tell me you're thinkin' about seein' Nicole right now.

*(**PETER** doesn't respond.)*

SULLY. I knew this was gonna happen. But don't worry, I'm prepared and rehearsed. Fuck *her* Pete. She betrayed you, she ain't worth it. And if tomorrow Nicole paralyzes you with her Medusa-like stare, tryin' to rekindle old shit, just gimme the nod and I'll pull ya out before you turn to stone.

PETER. Yeah Sully, listen –

SULLY. I know we've been through this ad nauseam and my hand to God – if Janice cheated on me I'm not sure what the expiration date would be on my dealin' with it. It's a justifiable thing to let linger. But fuck it, and fuck her because right now, as far as I can see, you've got a great girl in Carol. So you're not ready to propose – she's still great. Regardless, I got a better subject. I want – You're one of – Look at me, I'm like a teenage girl. Peter Patrick Callahan – I'd be honored if you'd be one of my groomsmen.

PETER. Sull – ah – yeah – course I will. Are you kidding me? The honor would be mine, man.

(They hug.)

SULLY. You know if I didn't have a brother, you'd be my best man.

PETER. Thanks Sull.

SULLY. A lotta people come in and outta people's lives and…you know…you're top notch Pete. Top notch. Cheers.

PETER. Cheers.

(They clink beers.)

SULLY. What are you drinkin'? An O'Doul's?

PETER. What?

SULLY. You've gone nonalcoholic on me? You in the program?

PETER. No.

SULLY. Then no. No no no. Not on Fitzy's weddin' weekend, not with an open bar on tap and me in town. You can wear your brassiere another day. Right now, we will, like old times, enjoy life through a beer-induced haze.

*(**SULLY** grabs Peter's O'Doul's and exits to the kitchen. He then reenters and hands **PETER** a Budweiser.)*

SULLY. Don't look so defeated for God's sake. I am not here to watch you drink some beer-flavored soda. I'm here to have fun. You gotta move back to Boston. I'm worried about you.

PETER. Here's to Fitzy getting hooked. And you, too.

SULLY. And you too someday.

PETER. Yeah.

    (They quaff a gulp from their beers.

    SULLY *takes note of Peter's expression.)*

SULLY. You're still in love with Nicole.

PETER. She was the best friend I ever had.

SULLY. The best friend who had an affair on you? I'm sorry Pete, but after she cheated on you, you couldn't form a coherent thought for months. Remember? This is me: "Hey Pete, you wanna get a beer?" This is you: "How did this happen? How did this happen? How did this happen?" Yeah, she's a great friend Pete. A good, great, *best* friend!

PETER. Does knowing you were wrong count?

SULLY. Call me old fashioned, but in a monogamous relationship there's certain things a woman shouldn't do. Lettin' another man insert his penis *into her* is one of them.

PETER. Sometimes people make mistakes.

SULLY. Some do, others don't.

PETER. I still love her. It's the truth.

SULLY. Is it? She's comin' to town. You're feelin' "feelings." "Stirrings." "Connections." Whatever you wanna call it Pete, she is your ex-girlfriend *for a reason* and you can't just black out all that shit 'cause time has healed, you know? Time heals bullshit. It makes you an idiot all over again is what time does.

PETER. I don't know about that.

SULLY. I do. There's plenty of shit that flies through the "feeling" realm, and just because it's a feelin' doesn't mean it's somethin' to *follow through on.* You gotta ask yourself if it's a feelin' that springs from, as you say, truth, or…temptation. Are you just tempted by memories of sunnier times? Half-remembered sex? The old memory libido is a potent liar.

PETER. We had the real thing Sull.

SULLY. Which makes it all the more disgustin' that she did what she did.

PETER. Haven't you ever done something you regret?

(**SULLY** *considers this.*)

SULLY. Crank called my Dad once.

PETER. There's things I regret.

SULLY. But if, like me, you went to church with your grandmother five days a week you'da stayed on the straight and narrow.

PETER. I've been to church.

SULLY. People come down on church. I look at it as AA for kids, except less sad and more singin'.

PETER. We should pitch that slogan to the Pope.

SULLY. I'm not sayin' I haven't had to apologize to the odd customer service rep for losin' my temper, but no, I don't have regrets. Not life alterin' ones. I'm glad to hear Nicole regrets droppin' her drawers and lettin' some other dude tap it, but hey –

PETER. If you did something drunk, and were full of remorse –

SULLY. Oh, and she "takes responsibility" huh? She "owns it?" What's that mean exactly? Sure, it sounds like she's doin' *somethin'* kinda, what exactly that is, who knows – distractin' you from the truth – regardless, it doesn't change what happened. She got fucked up, flirted, and decided to heave-ho everythin' you guys had for a romp on a some random fuck's futon.

PETER. I don't need to talk about this anymore.

SULLY. I do. It's my job to remind you. There's dos and don'ts pal. And if you do a don't, there's repercussions. And there, my friend, is the shortest class on morality you will ever attend.

PETER. Uh-huh.

SULLY. Nicole did a don't. She inflated an adolescent urge into somethin' she shouldn't have. That pursuit had consequences. Don't let her get all weepy with the

what-could-have-beens tomorrow. I can see it seepin'
in right now. You think I haven't wanted to get naked
with the occasional what-could-be now and then? I
have. But therein lies the truth. I just want to get it
on. Screw somethin' new. And yes, that may be a sign
of somethin', but if you take a step back you see that
some signs say STOP.

PETER. You always got points for poise, Sull.

SULLY. Poise nothin'. It's common sense. Desire is biol-
ogy. People get all aflutter tryin' to inject depth and
meanin' into it. Like when it arises it must be PUR-
SUED. Hogwash. If you want to live a life with some
tenderness and gravity, you can't get waylaid by some
juvenile temptation. Everyone has had fair warnin'.
Especially those of us who have had a Jesuit education!
Go back and re-read some novels, read some plays.
Every great story is about the consequences of fuckin'
someone you *shouldn't*. Oedipus. The Iliad. Romeo
and Juliet. Hamlet. If you inflate the wrong feelings,
and then ascribe to them the wrong kind of importance, shit *will* go down. It's designed that way. And
what she's gonna go through tomorrow, seein' how
much you're kickin' ass now, and realizin' she blew it –
that's her own self-inflicted sadness. Don't let it affect
you. If her sayin' "But I was drunk!" is the loophole she
needs to crawl through to look herself in the mirror
and move on, God bless, but don't get bogged down
in her wrestlin' with the *deserved* ramifications of her
mistake.

PETER. Life is more complicated than that Sull. I tip my
hat to you for your convictions. I'm in awe of that. But
you talk about church. I don't go anymore, but I still
got the big point. Sin is real. But sin can be forgiven. If
your regret is true.

(A beat.)

SULLY. *(joking)* Alright, don't go gettin' all deep on me here,
I've only had one beer.

PETER. Nicole was just – I've thought of nothing else the past two weeks. And I've gone round and round… and…it's still there. I know I need to be with her again. I need to try.

(A beat.)

SULLY. Or, forget everythin' I said, and work it out with her. *(joking)* Jesus, I put my back into that last ten minutes.

PETER. I appreciate your friendship.

SULLY. *(serious)* Just don't say you're "Followin' your heart." Include your head in the decision.

PETER. I am.

(A beat.)

SULLY. Well…Whatever you decide, I'll support you.

PETER. Thanks Sull.

SULLY. How do you even know Nicole –

PETER. She wrote to me.

SULLY. She was gettin' email in the Australian outback? I thought her whole goal was to go live off the grid.

PETER. She wrote me a letter.

SULLY. Wrote you a *letter*? Longhand?

PETER. Yes.

SULLY. *(giving shit)* With like a feather and an inkwell?

PETER. Ballpoint.

SULLY. She gets an "A" for effort. *(Beat.)* So you *did* know she was comin' to the weddin'.

PETER. I found out that day you called.

SULLY. So, basically, you've got until tomorrow *mornin'* to dump Carol so you won't feel guilty about tryin' to get back in bed with Nicole tomorrow *night*? *(Beat)* Sorry, it's the cop in me. Boilin' things down to just motive. Well. Thanks for waitin' until I got here. Should be a fun night.

PETER. It's not gonna be good.

SULLY. Why haven't you ended it with Carol yet?

PETER. She's been gone the past six weeks. She just got back today.

SULLY. What about the telephone?

PETER. She deserves more than that. Carol's been – It's – I'm really gonna hurt her.

SULLY. Yeah, Pete. But that doesn't make you a bad person.

PETER. I'll be sure to mention that to her.

SULLY. If it ain't right, it ain't right. You're not like this evil bad person because you figured out Carol's not the right woman for you. Just sucks to have to tell someone who has another thing in mind. But, that's life. Fun, fun, fun, deal. It's all a crapshoot until you take the vows anyway. You haven't got up on an altar and vowed in front of friends, family and God to honor and cherish her forever, right?

PETER. It's gonna suck.

SULLY. But Pete, you've never been afraid of the hard things. I admire you for it.

PETER. I'm not anyone to admire.

SULLY. I admire that you've found success down here after the shit you went through. I hate that you had to move to get away from the memory of Nicole, but I get it. Boston was soaked with memories of her, so you had to hack your way through that disappointment and start somewhere new. I don't know if I could have bounced back like you did.

PETER. You could.

SULLY. I haven't created a lot of wiggle room for instability. It's not my nature.

PETER. You learn things about yourself, you adjust.

SULLY. I have a masters degree in English and I'm a cop? Why? Fine, my masters is from a glorified community college –

PETER. Don't denigrate yourself.

SULLY. But really, why do I end up a cop?

PETER. Your father and your uncles were cops.

SULLY. I'm doin' nothin' with my degree *not* because I am incapable of puttin' it to its proper use, but because I am afraid to put stability at risk.

PETER. Stop.

SULLY. I want to have a family, and support that family, spend time with that family, coachin' sports and stuff – so what do I do? I take the only job with a pension that won't go belly up.

PETER. Why's that?

SULLY. Cops have guns. The people who manage our pension are more careful because of this. At least that's what I tell myself. *(Beat)* I'm not sayin' my job is easy, I'm sayin' that I couldn't take the licks you did and start over. And risk uncertainty. I'm engaged to the same girl I met sophomore year in high school. Like me, you had what you thought was *set.* Things went terribly wrong. You spun out. You're standin' tall now. I am in awe of *that.*

PETER. Don't be.

SULLY. And now you're talkin' about gettin' back together with the woman who set all that shit in motion? Well, if someone could make it work, it's you. As for lettin' down Carol easily, I got nothin'. I haven't been involved in a breakup since the 8th grade. And I was the dumpee. The dump-*er* was named Patty Quigley. Fuckin' bitch. Fuck, she fucked me up. Came back with a hickey from Jeff Colquit at the 8th grade dinner dance and just diced me. Ugh. What a slut.

JANICE. (O.S.) We're back!

(CAROL and JANICE enter carrying a grocery bag.)

CAROL. Alright, who could use another drink?

SULLY. Nobody more than you!

CAROL. Woo-hoo! Let's party!

(Blackout.)

Scene Four

*(Saturday morning. Chicago O'Hare Airport. **NICOLE** Connors, 29, is on her cellphone, leaving a message.)*

NICOLE. Hi. I'm in Chicago. Thunderstorms. I'm not landing until two now. It's pushing it with getting showered and all but, hell, if I have to go with wet hair, I go with wet hair, it's only Fitz. He won't care, right? One other thing. I changed my mind. Come meet me. We have to make up for lost time. Okay? Are we crazy?

Scene Five

(Saturday morning. Lights up as **CAROL** *walks in the door with two coffees.* **PETER** *walks into the living room, dressed for the wedding.)*

CAROL. Brought you a coffee.

PETER. Thanks.

CAROL. And sugar, because you're sweet. *(Beat)* I had a good time last night. Sorry I passed out. I haven't been that bad in a long time.

PETER. Carol.

CAROL. You have nice friends. I wish I could go to the wedding tonight.

PETER. Uh-huh.

CAROL. No, you're supposed to say, "I wish you could too," silly.

PETER. Carol, we, we need to talk.

(A beat.)

CAROL. About what?

(A beat.)

PETER. I'm – I'm unhappy.

CAROL. About what?

PETER. Carol, listen…

CAROL. About *us?*

PETER. I'm –

CAROL. What do you mean unhappy? How are you unhappy?

PETER. It's just that, I don't feel right.

CAROL. "Right," how?

PETER. I – I don't – it's, it's difficult to say –

CAROL. Peter, you're scaring me. That look on your face. Are you – you're not – are you breaking up with me?

(A beat.)

PETER. *(almost inaudibly)* Yes.

CAROL. Why? *(Beat)* Is this because I've been gone? Because
– because I'm back now and – I'm happy, really happy!
How can you be unhappy?

PETER. I'm sorry.

CAROL. Then why are you doing this to me?

PETER. Carol, I need –

CAROL. What? Tell me. Tell me what I can do to take away
the difficulty and make it less difficult – I – We can
work this out – what do you need? I don't wanna just
throw this away, I'm getting too old to throw things
away. We can – we can go see somebody, and talk to
them, and work this out.

PETER. It's not that easy to work out.

CAROL. It doesn't have to be easy, I can do hard. I really can.

PETER. It's not that. I know you can.

CAROL. I love you Peter. I love you. I want to spend the rest
of my life with you. I do – I, I –

PETER. Carol, I wish it wasn't this way.

CAROL. It doesn't have to be! This is where the work comes
in! Don't I deserve more than one "I'm not happy"
conversation?

PETER. You deserve somebody amazing!

CAROL. I think *you're* amazing!

PETER. I think you're amazing too. But I feel I need –

CAROL. *(vulnerable)* I have a lot to offer. Don't you – don't
you think I have a lot to offer? Because I do.

PETER. You have so much to offer…it's –

CAROL. What about Nantucket?

PETER. What?

CAROL. I'm sorry, I was looking for some shoe polish
because I had scuffed up my boots and I wanted to
look nice for your friends especially after I found the
reservation for the Bed and Breakfast and I thought
that maybe – Oh my God, I'm so stupid! It's for *someone else!* You're going with someone else! Have you
been cheating on me?

PETER. I haven't, I swear to you. I did make that reservation for you and I, awhile ago, and I – I wanted to go away but –

CAROL. Let's go away! Let's go away and be together just you and me, just you and me alone away from everything – just us.

PETER. Carol, I'm just not in a place where – I know this sounds – oh God, I don't know what it sounds like. I think, to try to be with you right now, just isn't right.

CAROL. Do you think it'll be right another time?

PETER. Carol.

CAROL. Think about it for a second!

PETER. I have!

CAROL. Peter, you haven't! You're stuttering and hemming and hawing! You don't know what you want, you can't make sense with what you're saying – you're just giving up! Take a second and think about it!

PETER. Carol, I'm sorry, I don't want to be in this relationship anymore. I don't love you.

(Silence. She's deeply wounded, but she has a quality of quiet strength as she gathers herself.)

CAROL. How depressing that you turned out to be so typical, Peter.

PETER. Carol –

CAROL. It's really some kind of unexpected drag. You there, looking down at your feet, me here, feeling like shit.

PETER. You're better off without me. You'll see, you may not see it now, but you will, you will.

CAROL. Do one thing at once, will ya? If you're gonna break my heart, do me a favor and spare me your forecast on my future. You bust up this thing we have – you, you – you – you take without warning this wonderful thing and you tear it down…and I'm supposed to do what now – just *shrug it off?* "Hey, we gave it a shot. No biggie." I've been in your life, you've been in my life, we spend most of our time together, doing things, talking about things – totally wrapped up in one another's emotional lives – and you're just gonna *upend* everything by stuttering through a conclusion you've come to all by yourself? You're gonna undo *ten months* with a quick conversation that kicks me to the curb? "Shuffle off! Bye-bye! Sorry you couldn't make me fucking HAPPY!" *(Beat)* Don't do this. Don't be this way. Tell me this is a joke. Tell me that you're not part of the shitty stuff in life, you're the good stuff like I thought you were. Tell me, tell me, tell me this is not going like this.

PETER. I'm sorry.

CAROL. How many women have you said that to your whole life? You trot out the sad face and try to look remorseful when inside you're like a kid on Christmas.

PETER. I'm not!

CAROL. I trusted you! I shared myself with you! I gave you a part of me no one else had ever seen. You fucking monster.

PETER. Carol, I'm not trying to be a monster.

CAROL. Then you've got a talent you weren't aware of 'til now. Fine. Go be alone. Drink some beer. Bang some chicks. Do whatever you gotta do that you think will make you *happy*. But while you're at it, grow up! You're twenty-nine! My father had a house, a career and three kids by your age. And I'm a great fucking woman! And you're scared of what I don't know, but I won't wait forever. So stop looking for happiness out there! Sometimes happiness happens through *effort*. Real love isn't just emotion, Peter. Sometimes it's an act of will.

(She leaves, and PETER *stands alone as the lights fade.)*

Scene Six

(Later that day. **CAROL** *enters Peter's apartment. She holds a shopping bag. She removes her coat. She places a set of keys on the coffee table. She removes a teddy bear from the shopping bag. She places it on the couch with a card. She feels a chill, and reaches for her coat, but sees Peter's coat, and puts it on. She smells it, taking his scent in. She sits on the couch. She puts her hands in the pockets of his coat. She pulls out a letter. It is Nicole's letter to Peter. She reads it. She looks up, seething, devastated, calculating. Lights down.)*

End of Act One

ACT TWO

Scene One

(Later that same evening. Lights up outside on a patio/balcony of a hotel in Manhattan. A wedding band is heard offstage. NANCY stands alone in formal wear.)

HENRY. *(offstage)* Nancy? Nancy!

NANCY. Henry, I'm out here!

(HENRY enters, wearing an oversized brown suit.)

HENRY. Hey hey, a little romantic balcony away from the crowd...

NANCY. Look at the Chrysler building!

HENRY. Got a nice glow to it.

NANCY. You got a nice glow going yourself.

HENRY. And it don't stop there Toots.

NANCY. Toots?

HENRY. Term of endearment.

NANCY. Uh-huh.

HENRY. And yet another endearing quality of mine is that I come with Sambuca!

(He pulls out a bottle of Sambuca from his suit.)

NANCY. Where did you get that?

HENRY. Just one of the many benefits of the open bar system.

NANCY. I guess we're gonna have to drink it.

(NANCY takes the bottle and swigs a huge gulp.)

HENRY. Where have you been all my life?

NANCY. Making mistakes with other people. Trying to live

51

them down.

(Awkward silence.)

HENRY. That question was more of a rhetorical –

NANCY. Let's play a drinking game!

HENRY. I gotta pace myself. I start rifling back shots, I'll be talking out my ass.

NANCY. When will I notice the change?

HENRY. You, my dear, are scrappy.

NANCY. You brought the bottle. It's a weekend of spontaneity. Let's drink. In college, we used to play "The get-to-know-you game." Simple. We trade bits of info. Each bit we do a shot.

HENRY. Is it too early to say I love you?

NANCY. Not if you don't mean it.

*(**HENRY** eyes her, confused.)*

NANCY. What's your favorite color?

HENRY. Brown.

NANCY. Drink.

HENRY. Simple game.

(Throughout the game they pass the bottle back and forth, swigging shots at the appropriate intervals.)

NANCY. Your turn.

HENRY. Before this, have you ever gone to a wedding with a guy you just met?

NANCY. No.

HENRY. Why me?

NANCY. That's two questions. You broke the rules. Drink.

HENRY. Complicated game.

NANCY. My turn. How many times have you been in love?

HENRY. Real times?

NANCY. You've *faked* being in love?

HENRY. No, but, "real" can be a very murky thing for people when it comes to love. There's high school love, which,

when people are going through it, they *think* it's real,
but then you look back and all it is, is just…puberty
juice. Then you got your basic college-love illusion,
where feelings are blown way out of proportion by
the fact that you can have sex somewhere other than
a car.

NANCY. Some people experience real love at that age.

HENRY. At that age people are in love with the idea that
they're in love. They like how it makes them feel
grown up. Then they're crumbled when it ends
because they realize it *wasn't* a real adult love. *(Beat)*
I'm gonna say that real adult love happens when two
people who have been completely devastated by either
of these delusions try to make a go of something new.
When two formerly heartbroken folks make a choice
to pursue new feelings for new people armed with the
knowledge of how much it could waste them. *That's*
love. Knowing the risk. Knowing it could blow up and
wreck you. But still diving in.

NANCY. Henry, you're avoiding the answer.

HENRY. What?

NANCY. How many real adult times have *you* been in love?

HENRY. Oh. Zero.

NANCY. That's depressing. Drink.

HENRY. I'm drinking.

NANCY. Doesn't that make you sad?

HENRY. I'm not gonna get all teary about it like it's some
big tragedy. Especially since all of my failed relationships have had one constant: ME. Regardless, one guy's
little personal romance thing doesn't really matter in
the big scheme of things.

NANCY. Who lives their life in the big scheme of things?

HENRY. Is that your –

NANCY. Rhetorical.

HENRY. Oh! Making up rules as we go!

NANCY. No, I'm just saying that people can't really live their life in the big scheme of things. Sure, it sounds great when you say it like it's the big *perspective-giving phrase* that's supposed to hinder you from articulating for more than a half second any disappointment you might have in the progress of your aspirations, romantic or otherwise, but isn't your personal life and how it's going the only consolation for all of the chaos the big scheme dishes out?

HENRY. Did you take a breath? Because I was worried there for a second. *(Beat.)* Look, you got world poverty on one hand, on the other my ragged unimpressive love life.

NANCY. But that doesn't mean it isn't important to you, right?

HENRY. Hey, what's with the interrogation?

NANCY. Just playing the game.

HENRY. Well, I've always found that introspection and fun are two great tastes that *don't* go together.

NANCY. Ask me.

HENRY. I don't want to hear about your old boyfriends.

NANCY. I'll keep it vague. C'mon.

HENRY. Uh, okay, how many times have you been in love?

NANCY. By your definition? Twice.

HENRY. See, that to me is like…Ouch. Unrecoverable, unfixable, deep…ouch.

NANCY. I'm over it. Besides, if it wasn't meant to be, it wasn't –

HENRY. Nancy, let's start a movement to kill off that familiar and overused lie. I understand the allure. But let's acknowledge that back in our separate pasts, whenever you or I were with people we liked, we wanted it to work out. But because of many choices made – some by us, some by others – we are here in this moment reaping an unexpected harvest, not because it is pre-ordained but because we had the guts to say yes to one date. And then we had the guts to say yes to another. And while it may not have been *meant-to-be,* it is. And it is an awesome *"is"* to be in the middle of…here with you, having a really nice time, on a spontaneous night.

(He swigs a shot.)

NANCY. We are having a nice time, huh?

*(They kiss. **PETER** enters, clearing his throat.)*

HENRY. Hey hey, Pedro!

PETER. What's up?

HENRY. Nancy – this is a great dude! You guys meet?

NANCY. You've introduced us three times Henry.

HENRY. Yeah, I'm like that.

PETER. You guys having a good time?

HENRY. Fucking ball Pedro!!

*(**HENRY** stumbles a bit as the Sambuca begins to take effect.)*

PETER. Careful Nancy.

NANCY. I can handle him.

PETER. Just keep him moving.

HENRY. Keep me moving baby! Keep me moving! Let's go dance!

NANCY. I thought you didn't like dancing.

HENRY. I had not yet met Signore Sambuca.

NANCY. Let me go to the ladies room and I'll meet you out there.

HENRY. Perfection.

*(**NANCY** kisses **HENRY** and exits.)*

HENRY. Ooo baby. You the man Pete! You the man! If you didn't float me that cash this may never have occurred! Thank you! Thank you my man! Thank you! *(Beat)* You think Fitz is pissed I just brought her along without an invite?

PETER. Nah, he's in his own world right now.

HENRY. Fitzy's married! Ha ha! Another one bites the dust!

Come on…come dance.

PETER. I will in a second.

HENRY. Saw you dancing slow with Nicole out there – she's looking sweet.

PETER. She is.

HENRY. Stranger than fiction my man. Stranger than fiction, you two. That's cool man. To be honest with you I always thought Carol was a hack.

PETER. She wasn't a hack, Henry. I really hurt her.

HENRY. Alright, that was uncalled for. I didn't – I didn't mean that. Actually, I did. I'm gonna – She wasn't a hack, she was – at the very least she must've done some hard-core narcotics as a teenager because she seems a bit squishy in the testa – *(Off* **PETER***)* You know what? Sambuca make me go ya-yo. *(Beat)* I'm, I'm gonna go detox.

*(**HENRY** exits. **PETER** stands alone for a moment. **NICOLE** enters.)*

NICOLE. Hey solitary man, out here all alone…You okay?

PETER. Just thinking.

NICOLE. All alone out here…I might have to take a little advantage.

(They kiss.)

NICOLE. Best lips ever.

(She scratches the back of his head.)

PETER. That feels good.

NICOLE. Can you believe it still feels like this?

PETER. I can. How ya holdin' up? Jet lagged?

NICOLE. Running on adrenaline. In a bit of a daze. But a good daze. Glad I came. Still a bit anxious.

PETER. Me too.

*(**SULLY** enters with a half-smoked cigar in one hand and a beer in the other. He's a little tipsy, but not drunk.)*

SULLY. Hey dudes, the party's indoors!

PETER. We're having a party right here.

SULLY. I can see that. *(Beat)* You lead an active life my man.

PETER. I'm happy.

NICOLE. We're both happy.

SULLY. So, this is happiness, yes?

PETER. It's the way things should be.

SULLY. You two together again actually looks good.

NICOLE. You approve Sully?

SULLY. Hey, I don't fight fate, I fight crime. You guys thirsty?

PETER. I could use one.

NICOLE. Where's Janice?

SULLY. Ah – she went back to the hotel, she was feelin' kinda ill I guess, I don't know. She started wiggin' kinda.

NICOLE. Oh. I'm sorry.

SULLY. What'll it be? Heineken? Bud? Or another one of those O'Doul-pussy-boy-beers you've been nipplin' all night?

PETER. Whatever's coldest.

SULLY. There's a problem drinker for ya. Watch him Nicole. He's gone downhill ever since you escaped to Australia.

(He exits.)

PETER. But I'm back on track now. Wanna take off?

NICOLE. Isn't it bad to leave before it ends?

PETER. It's almost midnight.

NICOLE. I know, but –

PETER. But what? We might miss Henry blow out his knee doing the limbo?

(She laughs.)

NICOLE. I missed you, Peter.

PETER. I missed you so much.

NICOLE. Let's go.

(They walk off, and a moment later, **SULLY** *returns.)*

SULLY. Yo! Pete? Nicole?

*(***HENRY** *enters. He's soaked with sweat from dancing. His jacket is off, and the bride's garter is wrapped around his left arm. He's drunk, but not completely incoherent.)*

HENRY. Sully! You fuggin' douche!

SULLY. Henry!

HENRY. You fuggin' douche! Fuck. There he is! Sully! Good to see you, you douchebag!

*(***HENRY** *hugs* **SULLY**.*)*

SULLY. *(amused)* Good to see you too Hank.

HENRY. I'm fuggin' looped! Woo! Ha-ha! Fuggin' great wedding.

SULLY. Not bad, huh?

HENRY. You're next!

SULLY. Damn straight.

HENRY. Baboom! Sully goes down! Crashin' and burnin'. Count the douchebag out! 10-9-8-

SULLY. It's gotta be done.

HENRY. I think it's fuggin' great. Really. Really. Fuggin' great.

SULLY. Thanks man.

HENRY. No, that's some cool shit dude. Cool shit…you're a good dude, Sully. I know we weren't real tight in college and shit but – I always kinda felt we were close… in the same *bracket* and shit, you know? 'Cause we both hung with Fitzy and Pete, you know…you know?

SULLY. Yeah.

HENRY. And fuck, you know. Fuck – it's just cool.

SULLY. Yeah, it is.

HENRY. And I really don't know Janice that well, but hey, you're a good man.

SULLY. She's a good woman. A catch. She really has a good heart. Sometimes too good for me.

HENRY. Don't sell yourself short Sull – that took some balls to work out.

SULLY. Relationships take work.

HENRY. Yeah, but you stayed friends with Pete too, you know? That's so cool.

*(**SULLY** finds Henry's drunken incoherence hilarious.)*

SULLY. You gotta find time in your life for friends.

HENRY. It's inspiring that you guys looked past that shit.

SULLY. Past what?

HENRY. You didn't let it dictate your course! You stared a shitty *shituation* in the face and dealt! But hey, honestly, that shit happens when people get loaded, you know?

SULLY. *(laughing)* Now what do you know about being loaded Henry?

HENRY. I know 'bout people, litsters, guys and dolls, they hook up and it's really not about anything other than animal instincts. We all have 'em. I got 'em. But mix the shit with booze and people gettin' all lit and shit and you know, talk about baboom. Ba-baboom. And it's cool you guys saw through all that, 'cause some people don't. They snap.

SULLY. Henry, I'm losin' you.

HENRY. You got down to the real shit! Which bottom line is about love. And feelings that – that are like nectar shit. Fuckin' marrow of life. You can't blow that shit off, even when things don't go according to plan. Don't get me wrong, Janice is awesome – fuckin' great girl – but really, *her and Pete?* It didn't go deep. It was *one random time.* Nothing more than your basic run-of-the-mill-drunken-slobber-fuck. You saw that. Too bad it took Nicole so long.

*(**SULLY** grabs **HENRY**.)*

SULLY. What the fuck are you talkin' about?

HENRY. Huh?

(**NANCY** *runs onto the balcony.*)

NANCY. Henry! The band's playing "The Hora!"

(**NANCY** *exits.*)

HENRY. At an Irish Catholic wedding?

(**NANCY** *returns.*)

NANCY. Henry, come on!

HENRY. Come on Sull! We'll put Fitzy up in that fucking chair! Then we'll drop him! It'll be a riot.

(**SULLY** *releases* **HENRY.**)

SULLY. No thanks, Hank.

HENRY. Okay. Fucking good talking to you Sull! You're a good dude!

NANCY. Henry!

HENRY. I'm coming! Come dance Sull!

(**NANCY** *and* **HENRY** *exit, leaving* **SULLY,** *alone, as his rage brews.*)

Scene Two

(Lights up on SULLY *and* JANICE *in their hotel room.)*

SULLY. You had to leave the reception because you were "sick" huh? Sick, 'cause you wanna fuck my best friend again, but he's taken?! That didn't stop ya before! I'll make you fuckin' sick!

JANICE. Steve, you're scaring me!

(He pushes her onto the bed.)

SULLY. Sit your ass down or I'll kick your fuckin' teeth out.

JANICE. Fuck you Sully!

SULLY. But not before you fuck Pete, huh?

JANICE. *Once,* drunk out of my mind! We knew it was wrong the minute we were done.

SULLY. But you didn't realize that when you were tryin' to get off, did ya?

JANICE. I was wrong.

SULLY. And I'm the big oaf that no one can tell the truth to?

JANICE. When Pete told Nicole she lost it.

SULLY. She left the country!

JANICE. And I knew you'd react the same way –

SULLY. I'm not done reactin'!

JANICE. Steve, it was a stupid mistake. A mistake made drunk and that doesn't make it right, I know. I was wrong, but – That night you and I got in a fight and you stormed out of my place and I went to find you but you had gone to Foxwoods to gamble. And I'm at your apartment, drunk, and Pete was there, and he was drunk, and we kept drinking, and then – it sounds so stupid –

SULLY. I wanted to have a family with you!

JANICE. I still do.

SULLY. Don't come near me.

JANICE. Steve, I was wrong, so wrong! I'm sorry! Steve, *you* mean something to me, not Peter! I want to marry you, not him!

SULLY. I cannot marry you and think of someone who was my best friend....Ahhhhhh! How could you do this to me, Janice? How could you let me fall in love with you and plan a whole life with you and then turn around and spit in my heart with this?

JANICE. *(pleading)* Steve, we can get past it. If Nicole and Peter can, we can too.

SULLY. You lied about our past. I don't live lies. So you can open your arms and lay on your back for somebody else for the rest of your life, because it sure as shit ain't gonna be me.

(He exits as the lights fade.)

Scene Three

*(Lights up on **PETER** and **NICOLE**, walking into his apartment later that night.)*

NICOLE. Nice place. Is it always this clean?

PETER. Not even close. Nicole, I am so –

(She cuts him off with a kiss.)

NICOLE. I just want to be in *this* moment. But, first, I wanna get out of this dress.

PETER. I don't have a problem with that.

NICOLE. This – this is a good thing.

*(**NICOLE** walks into the bedroom.*

***NICOLE** screams.*

***PETER** runs into the bedroom.)*

PETER. (O.S.) Nicole, get a knife! Nicole, in the kitchen! Hurry, Nicole!

*(**NICOLE** runs into the kitchen, grabs a knife and runs back into the bedroom.)*

PETER. (O.S.) Hold the legs! Hold the legs!

*(**PETER** carries out the limp body of **CAROL**, who has a noose around her neck.)*

PETER. Please, Carol, no, no.

NICOLE. Peter, who is she?!

*(**PETER** struggles with the noose.)*

PETER. I can't get this thing off!

NICOLE. Who is she?

PETER. There's a phone in the kitchen! Call 911!

(There's banging on the door.)

SULLY. (O.S.) Pete, open up! It's Sully!

*(**PETER** runs to the door and opens it.)*

PETER. Sully you gotta help me!

SULLY. How was it? Was it worth it?

(**SULLY** *grabs* **PETER** *and starts choking him.*)

NICOLE. Sully, it's not time to fuck around!

SULLY. *He's* the one who fucks around!

PETER. Sull, come on man.

NICOLE. Sully stop it! There's a dead girl here!

(**CAROL** *pops her head up.*)

CAROL. I'm not dead.

(**NICOLE** *screams.*

SULLY *is startled, but keeps choking* **PETER**.)

PETER. What the fuck?!

CAROL. How'd that make you feel you fucking asshole?

(**CAROL** *loosens the noose.*)

PETER. Carol, what the hell – you're sick!

CAROL. You're sick, you gutless asshole!

PETER. You're the sick one!

CAROL. You're the fucking asshole!

NICOLE. What is going on?!

(**SULLY** *finally releases* **PETER**, *who collapses on the floor.*)

SULLY. Nicole, how could you come back for this piece of shit?

CAROL. So this is Nicole!

NICOLE. Who is the dead-alive girl?

(**CAROL** *pulls out the letter, waving it in the air before she reads from it.*)

CAROL. You mean, "I want to try to recapture our love," Nicole? That Nicole? It's great how you dotted all the i's with hearts like I used to when I was *nine.*

PETER. Carol, you're fucking sick.

CAROL. You're a fucking scumbag!

PETER. You're a fucking sick twisted individual!

NICOLE. *(Baffled, not angry)* Peter, why does she have my letter?

SULLY. From Henry Pete! Drunk off his ass, that's how I find out?

(SULLY stalks PETER around the room.)

PETER. Sull – I didn't know how –

NICOLE. You never told him about you and Janice?

CAROL. What did he do to her?

NICOLE. Who is this? Who are you?

CAROL. I was your stand-in. For a year.

NICOLE. What?

SULLY. That's right Nicole, Pete gets around. When were you gonna get around to tellin' me you fucked my fiancee?

CAROL. You fucked Janice!?

SULLY. *(To CAROL)* Ahhhhhhh!

PETER. Sully, I'm sorry. I'm so sorry.

(SULLY grabs PETER in a headlock.)

SULLY. I am so tired of sorry. It's an empty, worthless string of letters that means absolutely nothin' to me.

PETER. I messed up Sull.

CAROL. Break his neck!

PETE/NICOLE. Shutup Carol!

PETER. I fucked up!

NICOLE. Sully! Please, it's Pete, you guys are friends.

SULLY. Friends don't fuck their friend's fiancees.

PETER. It didn't mean anything.

(SULLY releases PETER from the headlock.)

SULLY. What?

PETER. It didn't mean anything!

(SULLY grabs PETER by the lapels.)

SULLY. I loved her Pete! I loved her! How do you expect me to react to your sayin' it meant *nothin'* to you, but you still *did it*, because obviously it doesn't mean nothin' to me! Hell Pete, compliment me and tell me you had a thing for Janice *back then,* that you held a torch that was so all-consumin' that you finally, desperately, but with a heavy, hard heart decided to throw our friendship to the fuckin' dogs! Do me at least that fuckin' favor, huh?!

(**SULLY** *starts choking* **PETER.**)

CAROL. *(To* **NICOLE***)* You came back from Australia for this guy? You have to be crazy.

NICOLE. I'm not sure you're all there either, lady.

CAROL. I was all there 'til eleven o'clock this morning when he cut me off like a dead limb!

NICOLE. *(to* **PETER***)* What?

CAROL. He cut me off less than fifteen hours ago to prepare for the return of "Nicole," the great Nicole. What a pretty little letter from Nicole!

(**SULLY** *releases* **PETER** *into a crumpled, gasping heap, as* **CAROL** *rips the letter into pieces and throws it onto* **PETER.**)

NICOLE. Pete, why does she have the letter I wrote to you?

PETER. Carol, you're so fucked up.

CAROL. I'm fucked up? You're fucked up!

NICOLE. *(almost to herself)* This whole thing is fucked up.

SULLY. Did you know he told me that you cheated on *him,* Nicole?

NICOLE. What?

(**PETER** *crawls away from* **SULLY.**)

PETER. Sully, God help me. I was wrong – but I didn't know how to make up for it, and that's why I lied. I didn't know how to tell you, and I can't say anything to take it away.

SULLY. You can't take it away! You betrayed me!

(**PETER,** *on his knees, begs for Sully's forgiveness.*)

PETER. I know I did Sull. I betrayed my two best friends and after I told Nicole, she ran off to another country just to get away from me, and I – I didn't want to lose you as a friend too, I can't – I am so so so so sorry...

(**SULLY** *pulls out his gun and points it at his own head.*)

SULLY. What do you suggest I do now Pete? How do I get some – what do they call it? Closure?

(**SULLY** *stalks* **PETER** *around the room while holding the gun.*)

SULLY. Because Plan "A" was, I marry Janice and you're on the altar standin' next to me as my *closest friend.* But now Plan "A's" all shot to hell because of some soap opera bullshit that's awfully hard to choke down with a beer, a stinky stogie, and a couple of "I'm sorry's." So what's plan "B" Pete? What the fuck is plan "B?"

(**SULLY** *corners* **PETER** *on the couch.*)

PETER. I don't know.

SULLY. Open wide.

NICOLE. Sully!

(**SULLY** *pulls the trigger.*

NICOLE *screams.*

But the entire chamber is empty.

SULLY *releases an anguished yell, and pulls back the gun.*)

SULLY. For two years you've pretended to be my friend. I will *never* forgive you. You have completely altered my life. *(Beat.)* See, I lose my best friend and my fiancee in the same day, and it had nothin' to do with anythin' I did. Isn't that funny? I find that funny.

(**SULLY** *passes by* **CAROL** *and stops.*)

SULLY. *(to* **CAROL***)* You're a fuckin' psychopath.

(**SULLY** *exits.*

Silence.

Then:)

CAROL. You are so sad, Peter.

*(**PETER** is emotionally wasted.)*

PETER. *(softly)* Carol – I…What?

CAROL. Here I was thinking it was a me thing when it was really a *someone else* thing. Why couldn't you just say that?

PETER. Carol, I was trying to do a shitty thing the nicest way I knew how. I'm not worth this trouble.

CAROL. "I love someone else" is a lot different than "You don't make me happy." *(Beat)* Have fun on Nantucket. I hear it's great.

*(**CAROL** exits.*

*There's a long beat as **NICOLE** and **PETER** take in all that has just occurred. Slowly, **NICOLE** moves to pick up the pieces of the letter, placing them in a pile.)*

PETER. She must have found it in my coat.

*(**NICOLE** seems dazed, lost.)*

NICOLE. No one writes letters anymore. This was a sweet letter.

PETER. I kept it with me all the time. I read it over and over.

NICOLE. My mother use to say to me that when you write to somebody you put your soul on paper…

PETER. Nicole, I loved that letter.

NICOLE. My soul was on this paper.

PETER. I am beyond sorry.

NICOLE. You know what was the hardest thing about going away from you? When I left you I didn't want to leave you. Because I still loved you. Full blown, all the way. I mean, you're smart, and nice and handsome and funny. And really, I thought, a catch. And then that thing happened to us…

PETER. Nicole, I'm not just the person who made that

mistake.

(A beat.)

NICOLE. *(not angry)* When you told me about Janice and I couldn't handle it, I thought, okay, here's a chance for me to do some individual things, think through this. But even after I went away, the only thing that kept popping up in my mind would be your face. And I hated that. I hated that I couldn't forget you, because I wanted to…even though I still loved you. And you know what Pete? Most of the time, it hurt more to not be with you, than it hurt to think about what drove us apart. It almost would've been better to not know.

PETER. I thought being honest was the right thing.

NICOLE. But you weren't honest Pete! You told me, but you lied to Sully…you lied to him about me. What the fuck!? You told him *I* cheated on *you?!* Pete, what is that? Who are you?

PETER. I was a coward. I was a coward.

NICOLE. But it didn't stop there! You never told me that you were dating someone else! You never told your past to Carol – You dated that woman?

PETER. Yes.

NICOLE. For how long?

PETER. Ten months.

NICOLE. You're writing me all these letters, even though you've started something with someone else? Meanwhile, I'm walking around on the other side of the world, angry at myself for not being a forgiving person? What about all those letters that you wrote to me?

PETER. Nicole, I wrote to you because I felt those things! I still feel them! And I didn't know what else to do but convey that to you, and hope you'd forgive me one day, even though I didn't expect you to. I didn't start anything with her until a *year* after you and I split. I just met her one day, and one date became two, became a weekend, became a mutual vacation, became a relationship I didn't expect to be in...And then, you know – I'm not saying I did the right thing! I don't – *(frustrated)* ahhhhh! *(Beat)* You wrote me a letter two weeks ago saying you still loved me and wanted to try again...your first and only letter! A letter I thought would never arrive! Suddenly I was sent into a tailspin wondering what I should do and I looked at where I was with Carol, and thought, "I'm not with her because of love, I'm with her because I've been with her for a while, and all my friends are getting married, and she's a nice enough girl, maybe I should stick it out and maybe, just maybe, I'll fall in love with her." But that's not what it should be about. It shouldn't be about something that approximates the real thing.

NICOLE. I don't even know what the real thing looks like anymore.

PETER. Like us.

*(**NICOLE** grabs her coat, and heads for the door.)*

PETER. Where are you going?

NICOLE. We're not who we used to be.

*(**PETER**, desperate, grabs her.)*

PETER. Nicole, look, look – We can start from just today! The love that you have for me, that made you write that letter – that feeling you spoke about that was still alive in you, that's *once in a lifetime* stuff! Completely muddled by some fucked up shit, but it's here. And I don't mean to say fuck everybody else, but fuck everybody else! I don't care anymore. I have lived most of my life trying to be a good person and one stupid mistake left me in a place I had no skill in getting out of. And so I tried to do damage control but just fucked everything up. I'm not making excuses. It's inexcusable. For two years I've been trying to get myself out of the hideous place I had put everyone, but I just kept, sinking, sinking, and your coming back gave me a chance to put my life back on track with the destiny I knocked to pieces. Please Nicole, I want you in my life. I need you in my life. Maybe that's selfish. Maybe it's wrong to want that because of what I did, but please, please let me try to make things up to you. Let me prove to you that I'm more than the man who made all these mistakes. I know it's not easy to forgive, but we, you and me together, are right. We love each other. Love can conquer all!

NICOLE. That's what I thought too.

PETER. Please forgive me. Please forgive me for being a coward, because I'm trying to step up here! What do you want me to do? Because I will do it...I will do it, God help me, I will do it.

NICOLE. I want you to tell me why I lose the love of my life because of one drunken night? Because I don't know how you get back from there...I don't know how to get back. I don't know how to get rid of this thing... I thought I could, but it's...I thought...I don't know what I think anymore...

PETER. Nicole, these are the only things I know. I know I love you. I know we were put on this earth to be together.

NICOLE. Peter, I love you.

PETER. I love you Nicole.

NICOLE. But – I don't trust you.

PETER. Don't do this! You can't leave! I'm begging you, I'm begging you.

NICOLE. Peter, please, you're hurting me.

(He lets go of her. **NICOLE** *is sad, not defiant.)*

NICOLE. I have to go...

PETER. Nicole...

NICOLE. I have to go.

*(***NICOLE*** *stands still. Then she turns and walks out the door.*

PETER *slumps to the floor.*

The lights fade.)

Scene Four

(Light comes up on **SULLY** *and* **CAROL** *sitting on a stoop drinking beers covered in brown paper bags.*

Their shared sadness is evident.)

SULLY. Sorry I called you a psychopath.

CAROL. I never thought I was capable of that kind of rage.

SULLY. Oh, I saw the potential. But hey, I was pullin' up the rear on the psychopath scene tonight. I can go there easily. That's actually why I became a cop. Decided to turn a detriment into an asset.

(A beat.)

SULLY. Gotta say, pretty convincin' makeup job.

CAROL. Thanks.

SULLY. No, really. I've seen dead people. Where'd you learn how to do the noose, the movies?

CAROL. Yeah. I had a whole harness thing, under my shirt so I could, you know, hang there without actually...

(She trails off, lost in her grief.)

SULLY. Yeah? As far as the color scheme for a hangin' victim – and this is not a criticism – but maybe next time you might want to tone down the white makeup. Add a little more of a violet or a lilac hue. That's if – you know, you find yourself in a similar situation –

CAROL. It didn't look convincing?

SULLY. I think you got the desired reaction. Just sayin' that a little more purple couldn't hurt.

CAROL. Shit! I did all this research!

SULLY. Yeah, see, as you know, somethin' on film is one thing – to the naked eye...

CAROL. Goddamnit.

SULLY. It was great Carol. Really. I'm nit-pickin'. Look, I'll get you my contact info. If you need *anythin'* – like if you want to fake an overdose on your next boyfriend or somethin', I'll walk you through the morgue so you can pick up the nuances.

CAROL. Thanks.

(A beat. The chit-chat has not helped anything.)

CAROL. This sucks.

(A beat.)

SULLY. You pray?

CAROL. *(dazed)* Sorry?

SULLY. We Irish Catholic boys have always got a prayer handy, in cases like this.

CAROL. I gave up on prayers a while ago.

SULLY. That's because you haven't used *my* prayers.

CAROL. No, I don't think –

SULLY. Come on, work with me. It's a simple prayer.

(He makes the sign of the cross.)

SULLY. Repeat after me: *(Beat)* "Fuck 'em."

CAROL. What?

SULLY. Fuck 'em!

CAROL. Fuck 'em?

SULLY. It's not a question Carol. Fuck 'em!

CAROL. Fuck 'em.

SULLY. *(loud)* There you go! Fuck 'em!

CAROL. *(louder)* Fuck 'em!

SULLY. *(His real rage showing)* Fuck 'em!!

(A beat.)

SULLY. Feel better?

CAROL. No.

SULLY. It takes time. Takes a little bit of time. *(Softly)* Fuck 'em.

*(As **CAROL** begins to cry, she puts her head on Sully's shoulder. **SULLY**, welling up, stares out into the night.*

Slow fade.

Curtain.)

PROP LIST

ACT ONE

Scene One
A letter
Two cordless telephones
Carol's mobile phone

Scene Two
Black shoes
Brown shoes
Two wallets
A soda for Henry
One frequent flyer card
Two bank cards
A pack of cigarettes
Two menus

Scene Three
O'Doul's non-alcoholic beer
Budweiser
Cigars
Toilet paper

Scene Four
Mobile phone

Scene Five
Two cups of coffee
Four packets of sugar
Peter's coat
Letter from Scene One

ACT TWO

Scene One
Bottle of Sambuca
Cigar
Two bottles of beer

Scene Three
Large kitchen knife
Noose
Gun
Letter from Act One

Scene Four
Two beers
Two brown paper bags.

COSTUME PLOT

AUTHOR'S NOTE: All of the characters—Henry included—have enough clothing in their closets to look fashionable and decent regarding the occasion. In both of our productions we tried to restrain ourselves from *announcing* the individuality of the characters through their wardrobe. In other words, as we put together what the characters would wear, we tried to avoid statements such as "Sully's a cop from Boston, so he would *definitely* not wear this or that." Or "Henry's a novelist, so he *must* wear ripped jeans and a wrinkled shirt." Don't let the New York/Boston contrast or the cop/novelist/makeup artist personas get so extreme in their contrasting choices that they overtake the characters. These friends should still look like they belong together.   That said, do as you see fit. Below, I've listed some suggestions.

ACT ONE

Scene One:
SULLY:
Boston College T-shirt
Jeans
Sneakers

PETER:
T-shirt
Jeans
Sneakers

CAROL:
Jeans
Shirt
Sneakers

Scene Two:
PETER:
Jeans
Dress shirt
Suede boots

HENRY:
Jeans
Shirt
Shoes

SULLY:
Sweater
Shirt
Khakis
Rockport shoes

JANICE:
Fashionable brand of jeans
Fashionable top
Black knee-high boots

CAROL:
Fashionable headband
Fashionable brand of jeans
Fashionable boots

Scene Three:
NANCY:
Skirt
Blouse
Dress shoes

HENRY:
Sportcoat
Shirt
Jeans
Shoes

SULLY, JANICE, PETER, CAROL:
Same as Scene Two

Scene Four:
NICOLE:
Cargo pants
Cardigan sweater
Shirt Sneakers.

Scene Five:
CAROL:
Same as Scene Three

PETER:
Navy Blue suit
White Shirt
Green and Blue Tie
Black dress shoes

Scene Six:
CAROL:
Jeans
Shirt
Coat
Sneakers

ACT TWO:

Scene One:
HENRY:
Brown suit
Brown tie
Brown socks
Brown shoes

NANCY:
Dress
Low Heels

PETER:
Navy Blue suit
White shirt
Green and blue tie
Black dress shoes

NICOLE:
Dress
High heels

SULLY:
Black suit
White dress shirt
Red tie
Black dress shoes

Scene Two:
JANICE:
Pajamas

SULLY:
Same as Scene One

Scene Three:
PETER, NICOLE, SULLY:
Same as Scene Two

CAROL:
Hooded sweatshirt
Pants
Shirt
Sneakers

Scene Four:
CAROL and SULLY:
Same as Scene Three

ORIGINAL SET DESIGN

AUTHOR'S NOTE: The set, as described below, was a spectacular design that accommodated all of the scene changes despite the restrictions of money, time, and stage space. The stage we used at The Irish Arts Center was very small, yet we still wanted to have minimal movement between scenes and keep the changes quick. This was the designer Matthew Baird's greatest challenge, and he rose to the occasion brilliantly. What follows is his plan, which served us well.

"Diverting Devotion" Set
By Matthew Baird

The stage set was conceived as an armature. In the same way that a wire framework supports a sculptor's clay, this set would act as a structural support for action being added to the stage. By keeping its elements abstract in their references, the backdrop is able to accommodate the multiple settings which occur in the play: An apartment, an automobile, a hotel room, an outdoor wedding reception, and a cafe. The goal of the design was to support all of these actions using only light and depth for division, rather than mimetic props...

The armature subdivides the stage front to back into three spaces on stage right, and two spaces on stage left. These spaces at stage right provide the intimate terrace scene, the cafe scene and the more distant automobile scene, as well as the obscured depth of Peter's bedroom. Stage left spaces are dedicated to Peter's kitchen and living room. For the automobile scene we used an actual steering wheel that Sully carried out with him, which accented the setting...

Divisions are made between these spaces by employing overlapping planes of scrims and flats which also serve to create the illusion of varying depths and intimacies. To increase the illusion, both sidewalls are skewed in a forced perspective. A hinged scrim cantilevers the sidewall of stage right, out over the edge of the stage, blurring the boundary between audience and players. During the Second Act, the scrim hinges back parallel to the stage edge to provide the backdrop for the moonlit terrace scene.

1. Back stage/dressing area
2. Peter's kitchen
3. Prop storage shelf
4. White shark tooth scrim on gray painted wood frame
5. Wood counter top w/ wood bar stools
6. Front door
7. Peter's living room
8. Car scene/ hotel scene
9. All side walls flat battleship gray
10. Bistrotable/ Restaurant scene
11. Hinged scrim panel
12. Fold down bench for wedding scene
13. Stage floor painted flat black
14. Rectangular area painted high gloss red
15. Sand-blasted glass coffee table
16. Modern leather couch and chair
17. Black out curtain
18. Flip down seat converts car scene to bed scene

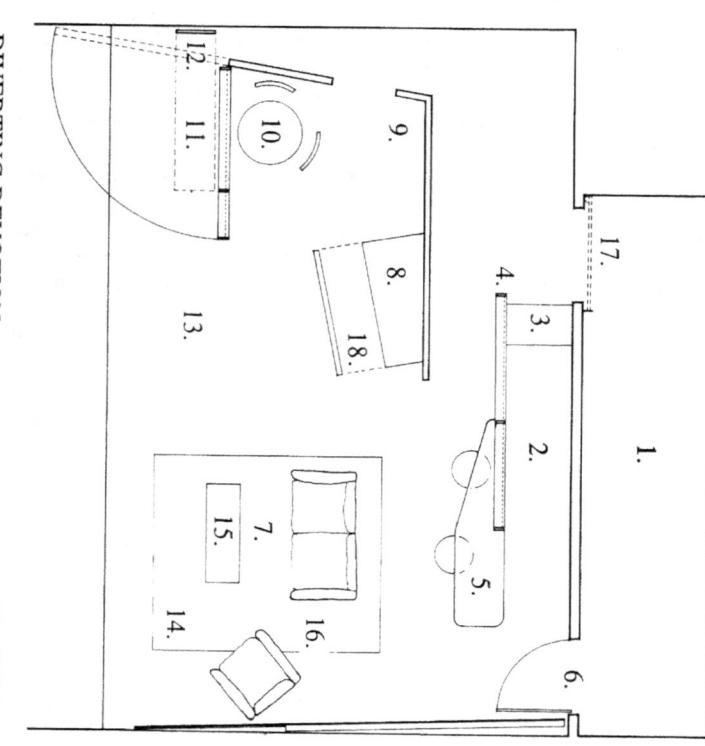

DIVERTING DEVOTION
Stage Plan

0 1 2 4 ft

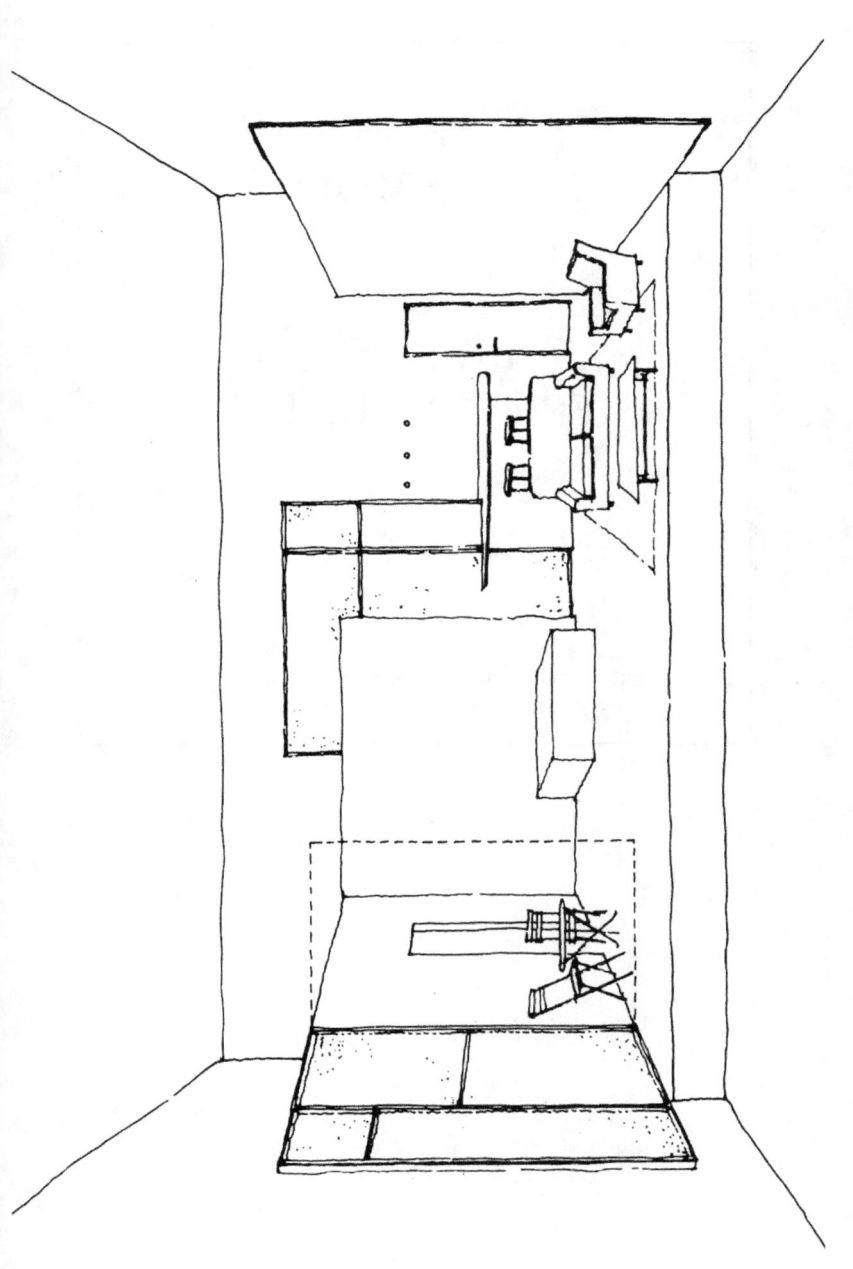

Also by
Mike O'Malley...

THREE YEARS
FROM "THIRTY"